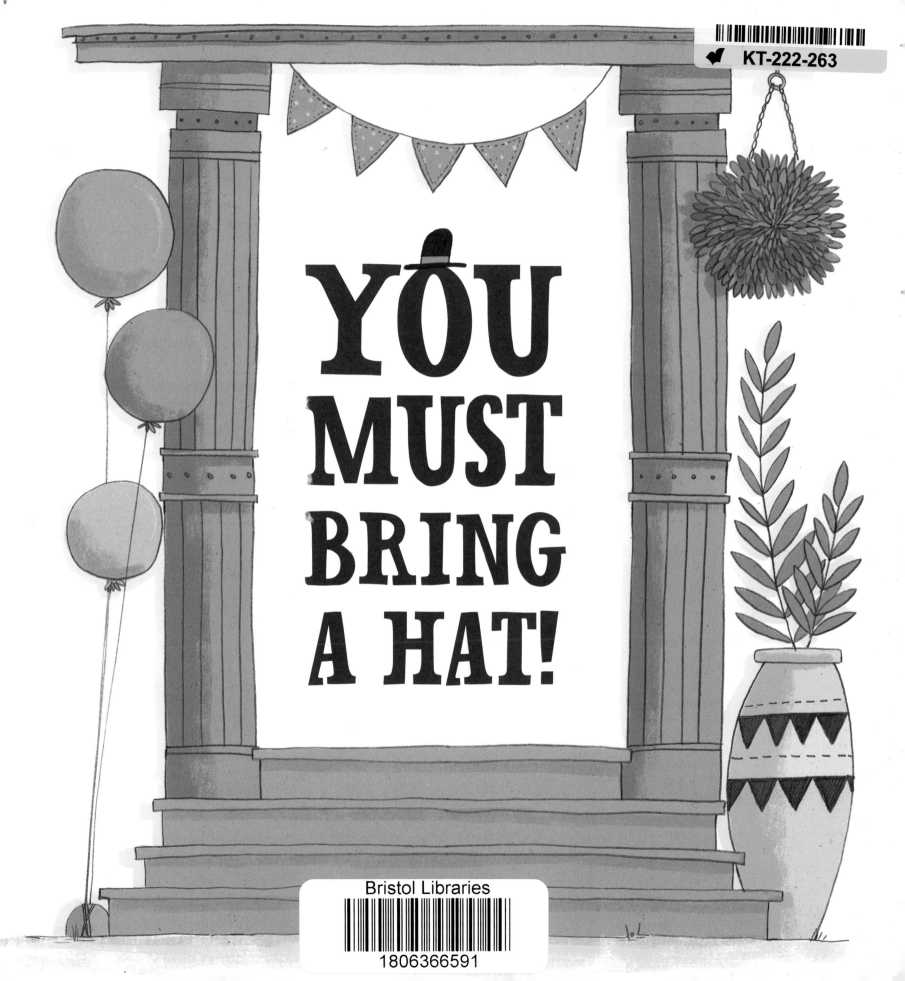

YOU MUST BRING A HAT!

For Mum and Dad, thank you for everything x - SP

For Nia, a massive thanks for all your help! - KH

**SIMON AND SCHUSTER**
First published in Great Britain in 2016 by Simon and Schuster UK Ltd
1st Floor, 222 Gray's Inn Road, London, WC1X 8HB · A CBS Company · Text
copyright © 2016 Simon Philip · Illustrations copyright © 2016 Kate Hindley
The right of Simon Philip and Kate Hindley to be identified as the author and
illustrator of this work has been asserted by them in accordance with the
Copyright, Designs and Patents Act, 1988 · All rights reserved, including the
right of reproduction in whole or in part in any form · A CIP catalogue record
for this book is available from the British Library upon request.
978-1-4711-1731-2 (HB) · 978-1-4711-1732-9 (PB) · 978-1-4711-4396-0 (eBook)
Printed in China · 10 9 8 7 6 5 4 3 2 1

# YOU MUST BRING A HAT!

Simon Philip
& Kate Hindley

**SIMON AND SCHUSTER**

London  New York  Sydney  Toronto  New Delhi

I received an invitation to a party.

YOU ARE CORDIALLY
INVITED TO THE
BIGGEST, BESTEST
**HATTIEST**
PARTY OF ALL TIME

Starts at 5·30pm

Wide brim house, 32 Panama avenue, west trilby

You may bring as many extra guests as you wish but you MUST bring a hat.

Kindest regards,

Nigel (host and fanciest hat judge)

P.S. seriously, don't forget the hat, the party depends on it.

P.P.S. try not to be late this time.

Immediately I panicked.
I DIDN'T OWN A HAT!

And the invitation specifically
stated that I MUST bring a hat.

The party depended on it.

I searched everywhere for a hat.

But the only hat I could find belonged to a monkey.
"That's a lovely hat. Can I borrow it please?"

"No."

"I really, really need a hat for a party. I'll give it back."

SIMIAN SID'S
SUPERIOR
S·A·U·S·A·G·E·S

As he wouldn't negotiate,
I was left with no choice . . .

At least I had a hat. Even if it
was still attached to a monkey.

But on arrival, the security was pretty tight.

**"Invitation please,"** said the doorman.
Apparently there were other rules too.
**"Sorry Sir, but we're under strict instructions
not to let in any hat-wearing monkeys . . .**

**unless** they are also
**wearing a monocle."**

Luckily, we soon bumped into a badger named Geoff.
He was just the sort of badger we required.

*"I do beg your pardon chaps,
but are you, by any chance,
after a monocle?"*

"Indeed we are.
We need it for a party."

*"I will lend this monkey my monocle on the condition . . .*

*that I may accompany you to your shindig."*

**"Invitation please,"**
the doorman said again.

**"Sorry Sir, but we're under strict instructions
not to let in any hat-and-monocle-wearing monkeys
if they are accompanied by a badger called Geoff . . .**

**unless Geoff
can play the piano.”**

“Can you play the piano?” I asked.

*“Don't insult me.
I'm a badger!
Of course I can.”*

"Geoff can play," I said firmly.

**"I'm afraid we need to see that," the doorman replied.**

Geoff was good.
But we still had a problem.

**"Sorry Sir, but we can't let this piano-lending elephant in.
He's not wearing a tutu."**

Just typical! There's NEVER a tutu around
when you need one.

We sorted that problem surprisingly quickly.
Surely NOW we'd be allowed in?

But we'd failed to notice the sign.

Ah.

Martin kindly helped us out. And, as he was a very clever penguin, we were already prepared for the next rule:

**"All penguins accompanying pink-tutu-wearing elephants MUST bring with them a suitcase full of cheese."**

But it turned out the cheese needed to be sliced,
and none of us had thought to bring a knife.

And that was when I broke.

"LOOK, THESE ARE THE SILLIEST RULES I'VE EVER HEARD. NIGEL CLEARLY INVITATION THAT I COULD BRING SO LONG AS I BROUGHT A HAT A MONKEY IN A HAT SO I BROUGHT A HAT

...STATED ON HIS ... ANYONE I WANTED ... AND I BROUGHT ... TECHNICALLY ... AND ..."

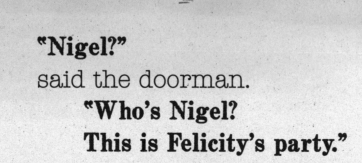

"Nigel?"
said the doorman.
**"Who's Nigel?
This is Felicity's party."**

"This isn't number 32?"

**"Next door."**

Oops.

Still, Nigel's party was worth the hassle . . .

Even if we were a little late.